# SHERLOCK HOLMES
## URBAN FANTASY MYSTERIES 2
# JOHN PIRILLO

Copyright 2022

# Magic

# Incident at Foulinsworth

"**L**adies and Gentlemen, I give you the most dynamic, creative and powerful performer of our times..." the Announcer said from the front of the huge stage set in the Foulinsworth Hall, a place where even royalty came to see performances. Stars from every generation also came to mix with royalty and to watch new stars rising to prominence.

It was a gay time for all.

Apples covered with sticky molasses, pear slices dipped in thick brown sugar, candies of every color and shape...from truffles to hard chocolates, both milk and dark...were sold to an audience eager to forget the world outside and live for a time in imaginary worlds wrought by great actors, stage magicians and high wire acrobats.

Cherry Barns, one of the lighting directors for the hall, listened to the Announcer, a smile touching his lips. He always felt excited at such times. Even nervous. While not the star of the show, his performance with the lights was just as important to its success as the man who would be performing...Harry Houdini!

So, Cherry sat on the spider work crossbeam where the Tesla spots were arranged to light the stage, wiggling his toes. He never climbed this high in shoes. Too easy to slip and fall. He still remembered his old friend Carrington who had gotten all the way to the top, only to slip on the top rung of the ladder because he wore shoes, when he hastened to put his foot again on the rung, instead had caught the shoestring of his other shoe and when he lifted that foot, had lost his balance and tumbled head over heels to his death.

So, Cherry had made it a point from then on to not climb the ladder, but to use the hatch in the stairwell and walk across the beams instead. He was light on his feet and sure footed. He also had no fear of heights, so was not worried on that account.

Cherry had a glass of wine on the beam next to him. He never drank more than one small sip. And it was always in memory of his lost friend and mentor. Carrington had taught him all the tricks of the trade, including how to shock the royal jewels off someone if they were not playing fair.

"To you Carrington," he said in a light voice, raising his glass of wine.

But when he went to drink it; it was empty.

"What?" He gasped, looking at the empty bottom of the glass.

"Impossible!" He exclaimed.

BELOW, THE ANNOUNCER strode forward, almost touching the knees of a beautiful blonde-haired Duchess, who always sat in the same spot. Lady Carolina.

He did not smile at her; but she smiled at him, and unseen by the audience, placed her delicate right foot over his booted one and pressed lightly, letting him know she was available.

His face lit up as he spoke. The audience thought it was because he was so excited to announce the performer, but it was because the blood was rushing to the various parts of his body in anticipation of the later hours when the show was over, and the Duchess was keeping him warm and cozy.

Her husband, the duke, never spent evening at home. He always had a mistress somewhere about town that he slept with...discretely of course, but everyone knew anyway. The truth always comes out in the end, he thought with an amused smile, never once entertaining the thought that it might about him as well. But such are humans that they predict the lives of others but fail miserably at their own.

Once again, the bright smile on his face of amusement this time was mistaken for further excitement. The audience thought him only excited about the words he was about to announce. But it was not.

"Ladies and gentlemen, I give you the one and only, the world's greatest stage performer and magician...Harryyyyyyyyyyy Houdini!"

CHERRY SWUNG THE BRIGHTEST Tesla offstage, caught the slender, muscular figure of Harry dressed in his sequined outfit, and followed him on stage with it, keeping it centered about him.

HARRY WAS WEARING A skintight outfit, which was covered with semi-precious stones polished so highly that they reflected the light back in every direction. He was a peacock of light as some of his fellow performers teasingly pegged him.

The audience oohhh and ahhhh, clapping as he stepped to center stage and took an enormous and graceful bow.

He straightened up.

The audience hissed at one another for quiet.

The Announcer waited.

Finally, when the audience was settled, Harry nodded to the Announcer, who said, "Mister Houdini, the world's greatest magician, will tonight vanish before your very eyes and return riding a dragon."

The audience became extremely excited.

"A living dragon," the Announcer shouted over their voices.

The audience gasped. No longer excited in the way of before, but now wary, because dragons were known to be vicious creatures that would burn anything and everything down if angered or upset.

Again, Harry nodded.

The Announcer brought a pistol, which he had hidden in his jacket upwards and fired six blanks, shattering the sudden silence.

The lights from overhead went twirling about the stage and into the audience, creating a kind of brief chaos before their colors changed to extremely warm tones about Harry.

At first there had been screams of alarm, and then the audience dropped into a shocked silence as Harry walked straight forward to the edge of the stage, smiled, and then said, "I want you to be sure that your eyes never leave me. Not even once. For the magic I am about to perform can be missed if you do so and you will surely be frightened to death when I come back with the dragon."

More alarmed sounds, some women, and men, hastily getting up to find a bathroom to relieve themselves. That is how frightened they were.

Harry raised both arms, the bright material flashing light and sparkles all about the theater, raising both smiles and surprised looks.

"First, I shall perform what must be considered as a base move before I progress to the true magic and..." he grinned, "...the dragon!"

More ooohhhs and ahhhhs from the audience.

He moved his hands in a cycling motion and as he did, so cards began to appear between his fingers, shifting between one finger and the next to the other hand and back.

The audience leaned forward trying to figure out what he was up to.

Harry brought his easily. The deck of cards began to slide up his arm towards his face. He dropped

his chin and then blew on them as they arrived.

Each card would fly off and then boomerang back into his left hand, until he had a full deck once more.

He held the deck up.

The audience clapped politely. It was a lovely trick, but they had seen better.

Harry then grinned brightly, and the deck of cards suddenly exploded away from him in every direction.

The audience was so startled by the sudden, loud whoosh of the cards and their flying towards them, that they did not realize Harry had vanished until the cards fell to the stage floor and the theater floor and remained still.

"He's gone!" A man in the fifth row shouted.

"But how?" The Duchess asked politely to the Announcer, who winked and said, "Wait for it."

She nodded.

The audience began calming down, but this time something even stranger happened. The cards that had flown all over the theater suddenly rose back into the air and flew towards the stage, revolving around each other, creating a large cloud of interwoven movement.

Then the cards exploded in a huge balloon of fire.

The audience jumped to its feet, fearing this was not part of the act, but the theater catching on fire.

Before they could move an inch, the fire parted and Harry's face peeked through the plumes of the fire and then a huge spread of wings spread from the sides of the fiery holocaust and a dragon stepped into view with Hairy on its head.

The audience stood there shocked and stunned. Not moving an inch.

Harry rose until he stood exactly on the dragon's snout. "Now, the real magic begins."

He raised his arms.

"I am going to perform a trick never before attempted. One that no man, no magician has ever tried and survived to talk about it," Harry explained loudly.

The Duchess without thinking about it clenched the Announcer's right hand.

The audience did not notice. They were just as enthralled, mesmerized, and surprised as the Duchess by what he had said.

Harry lowered his body, the muscles in his legs bulging as he gathered his strength for a leap. The dragon, meanwhile, eyed the audience hungrily, making many of them nervous, and then it opened its mouth, as if ready to gulp someone down.

Harry sprang into the air and did a swan dive...straight into the gaping mouth of the dragon.

The dragon shut its jaws.

The audience screamed and gasped in horror.

"Harry's dead!" A man in the upper balconies cried.

"The dragon will kill us all!" A woman screamed.

The Announcer ignored the shrill complaints and fears and delicately unwound the hand holding his. "Wait for it," he whispered to her, when she started to give him an angry look.

"Wait for..." she began.

The dragon suddenly opened its jaws as wide as it could and bellowed out a huge fireball that shot for the ceiling.

The audience cried out in terror, but then when the dragon did not budge further, and the flames vanished. They saw Harry clinging to a rafter above by his strong arms, his muscles bulging from the effort.

The Announcer smiled, and then said. "I give you Harry Houdini, the greatest Magician in the World!"

The audience broke into loud cheers, rose to its feet, and gave Harry thunderous applause.

Harry began swinging hard back and forth and then let go.

The dragon stood up on its back legs and opened its mouth again.

Harry dove straight into its mouth.

The dragon folded its huge wings about itself, and an explosion of light shook its form and it vanished, leaving behind a huge pile of gray ashes where it had stood in the shape of a dragon.

The audience stood in shock, not knowing what to think.

Where had Harry gone to?

Where was the dragon?

Then the ashes began to move.

Some women fainted.

Several men ran way.

Then a pair of well-muscled arms poked out and Harry Houdini stepped from the ashes to the apron of the stage. The Announcer walked forward with a wet towel, which Harry used to wipe the ash from his face.

He bowed to the audience and remained bowed.

The audience broke into applause that did not stop for a whole hour.

CHERRY ROSE FROM HIS seated position to begin flicking off the Tesla spots. As he did so he felt something behind him.

He turned about.

THE AUDIENCE STOPPED clapping and began shouting in terror and screaming when Cherry, his voice etched with extreme pain and terror fell from above, his body alight like a flaming torch.

# Sherwood Forest

Dawn hung above the forest like a golden ripe melon ready to burst and spread its warm juices. Merlin and Harry walked a broad path littered with freshly fallen elm leaves and fast-growing grass and moss. The grass was moist from the morning dew and green and golden from the light of the morning sun.

The sun itself hovered like a shy intruder, just above the tree line. It cast tentative fingers of gold and red among the thousands of fluttering leaves above the two.

To Harry at that moment, he felt like he was walking through one of those magical forests like those that existed in Fairie, which Merlin sometimes told him about on a quiet evening.

Harry and Merlin halted once as a flight of birds arose from a nearby bush, calling out in alarm, "Humans, humans!" Of course, Harry could not be sure that is what they said, his ability to understand birds was not that developed yet, but he was getting there.

But even the birds, seemingly frightened by the sounds of Harry and Merlin treading upon fallen leaves and tiny branches, making crackling, and crunching sounds, seemed to sense the specialness of this morning.

They sang to each other in bright songs and harmonies that rose and fell like gentle fingers of sound upon Harry's ears.

The sun barely peeked through the high mantle of the overgrown forest, but where it teased the ground with golden fingers, the ground rewarded the light with sparkles and glows of diverse colors natural to the materials found there.

"It's beautiful, Merlin," Harry sighed.

"Yes, deceptively so," Merlin replied.

Harry, who was a young man at that time, barely past his middle teens, gave Merlin an inquiring look.

"You see, Harry, not everything is always as it seems. Certainly not as it appears."

"I don't understand, Merlin."

"Stop!" Merlin ordered and Harry froze at the sharpness of the warning, stunned.

Merlin struck the ground to Harry's right with his staff.

A slender snake rose and hissed from beneath the leaves piled there and struck at the staff.

Realizing it was just wood; the snake backed off and slithered away.

"Had you continued on the path you were, that viper would have struck your ankles."

"I hate snakes," Harry said, edging behind Merlin.

Merlin laughed. "Believe me, Harry; they hate man as much as man hates them. Neither one genuinely loves the company of the other. The snake because man steps on him and treads upon him with their carriages, cows, and horses. The man because the snake seeks the warmth of his home and sneaks through cracks of the wood to bed itself there and then bites when frightened or alarmed."

"It's an uneasy alliance between nature and man," Harry thought aloud.

"Perhaps, or maybe there are other factors that determine the course of events between a snake and a man."

"You act as if snakes were somehow intelligent," Harry complained.

Merlin laughed. "Harry, sometimes they are more so. But mostly, you are right, snakes are guided by divine laws, as is all of nature, but laws can be broken."

Harry saw the sad look on Merlin's face. "Man causes that, doesn't he?"

"I am afraid so. Man, blithely goes about smacking the heads of nature's creations, never once asking if that was meant for him to do, but rather reacting blindly to his emotions."

"Like my teacher sometimes strikes me on the knuckles when I don't remember my words properly?" Harry asked.

Merlin snickered. "I rap your knuckles because you keep trying to dip them into the cookie jar when you should be listening!"

Harry laughed. "Got me there."

Merlin smiled.

Merlin chuckled. "Have you ever had to waken a sleeping snake?"

Harry shook his head. "I'd rather not have that opportunity, if you please, sir."

Merlin laughed and clapped a hand on Harry's shoulder. "Neither would I, but sometimes one must grasp the snake before it grasps you."

"You mean bite, don't you?" Harry asked.

Merlin did not reply. He just kept walking.

# 221B Baker Street

Ms. Hudson walked casually along the sidewalk, both hands holding cloth bags filled with groceries. She spotted her flat and headed for the stairs.

Suddenly, she stopped.

"What was that?" She asked, shuddering.

She looked up, then to her right.

Something flits from view in the window of the flats opposite her own. She kept watching, but it did not return, whatever it was. She shivered, then shrugged and went up the stairs to her front door.

Before she could reach it, the door flung open.

She let out a startled cry and backed up, almost tumbling from the porch.

Watson caught her and grinned. "I'm keeping you off balance, am I?

She shook her head at his corny humor, and then he grabbed her bags and headed upstairs. She paused for a moment at the entrance to look back out.

What was it that kept bothering her? She wondered. She sighed with frustration, and then smiled at the thought of Watson waiting for her to give her a hug.

MS. HUDSON SET HER knitting gear down by her favorite chair, and then sat herself down. She pulled her shawl about her shoulders, preferring that warmth rather than the fire blazing in the hearth.

She picked up her darning needles and string and began knitting. She was working on a potholder. It was shaping to look like a four-leaf clover with a beautiful red rose in its center.

"Quite lovely, Ms. Hudson," Holmes complimented her from the table, where he had a cup of coffee at hand, which he had set down to speak to her.

"Thanks, Holmes. How are you this morning?"

"Busy as always."

She eyed the table. Nothing, but the coffee sat there.

He smiled.

She turned her attention back to the knitting. "Oh, then nothing's afoot?"

"Oh yes, very much afoot," Holmes announced. "Harry is about to knock on the front door, and he has rather somber news."

A knock on the door below.

Watson rushed from his bedroom and down the stairs to open the door.

"Harry," he greeted. "What brings you here this early in the morning?"

Harry entered and shivered once. "The devil's work I'm afraid."

Watson lost his smile.

Harry and Watson climbed the stairs quietly, each thinking about the meaning of the words...but in entirely different directions.

"Come in, Harry," Holmes greeted before Harry could step into view.

Harry came into the sitting room, and then nodded to Ms. Hudson. "Good morning, sweet lady."

Ms. Hudson smiled at him. "You're up early."

"Business at hand," he replied to her a bit tersely.

She gave him a surprised look.

He went to her and gave her a light brush of his lips across her forehead. "Please forgive my brusqueness, dear lady, I am tortured at the moment and my emotions ran over my ability to control my mouth."

She laughed and shoved him away. "John, can you fetch some fresh coffee for Harry, I am almost done with my knitting. If I set it down now, I will lose my thought."

Watson nodded. Then went down the stairs.

Harry came to the table and sat down next to Holmes.

Before he could speak, Holmes did, "Your show did not go well last night, did it?"

Holmes leaned forward and investigated Harry's face.

"You have not slept a wink."

"Not a one," Harry admitted.

"It wasn't your demonstration; your feat of magic that depresses you."

Holmes looked closer at Harry. "Someone close to you died."

Harry gave Holmes a surprised look.

"How could you know that, Holmes?"

Holmes scrunched his eyebrows together as he continued. "Beneath the fingernails of your right hand are traces of blood. The left hand looks burnt, as if you were trying to put out an extremely hot fire. You failed."

Holmes looked into Harry's eyes.

"It was someone who fell from above."

"Correct, but..."

"They were your electrician...no, your lighting man. Cherry, his name was."

"Holmes..."

"You were at the end of your act...hence still wearing your costume beneath your cloak and jacket...and he fell near to you.

"You rushed to try and save him from the fire consuming his body, hence the burns on your hands, the scorched hair, and the smell of smoke on your clothing. He meant a lot to you."

"How could you know that, Holmes?"

"Because you forgot to use a protective spell when dealing with the fire. You only do that when your emotions take over. Thereby, my line of reasonable deductions which I have heretofore administrated to you."

Harry slumped on his chair, his face suddenly dark and miserable looking, the brighter, cheerier look gone.

Holmes gave Harry a sympathetic look.

"It seems that fame dogs your footsteps, Harry."

"This kind of fame I can live without. I lost a friend. They are irreplaceable."

Before Holmes could say more, there was new knocking on the door.

"Who now?" Ms. Hudson asked, surprised at more visitors.

"That will be Conan and Challenger. No doubt they heard about the death this morning in the papers where it will have been prominently headlined on the front pages."

"But how did you know that?" Harry asked.

Watson came into the room and threw down the morning paper with the headlines declaring the death at Harry's performance.

Harry gave Holmes a scowl.

Holmes spread his arms and smiled.

# 221B Baker Street

"And that's when I realized that Cherry had been brutally murdered," Harry explained to Holmes and Watson, who sat at the table, listening intently.

Challenger and Conan sat on the sofa; their eyes focused inwardly as they considered the implications of the death.

Conan broke the sudden silence.

He stroked his fine mustache several times, and then said, "But Harry, how could the man have just burst into flames like that?"

Challenger scowled at Conan. "He was minding the electronics, Conan. Those can burn the skin right off your body if not handled properly," he pointed out.

"True," Harry agreed. "But Cherry was nowhere near any kind of power terminal with that amount of amperage to do that, Conan."

"Then what could have caused the fire?" Conan demanded.

Watson glanced at Holmes, who was quietly smoking his pipe, his eyes unfocused.

"Holmes?"

Holmes set his pipe down in its holder, and then folded his hands in front of him on the table. "Harry, this has all the markings of Lovecraft."

"Magic then?" Watson asked.

"Dark magic," Holmes replied.

Holmes rose. "Harry, is it possible that your magic, the one you used to carry you between our world and Fairie, created a vacuum? Sucked into our world one of the monsters that lives there?"

"Anything's possible, Holmes, but I would have sensed it if something had followed me back."

Holmes grinned. "But what if you were not followed?"

Harry gave Holmes an inquisitive look for a moment, and then his eyes lit up. "Did something exit with us? Directly then?"

Holmes said, "Perhaps that, or something was waiting for the opportunity to reveal itself at your most weak moment."

"But that would mean that it rode my magic," Harry gasped.

"Perhaps," was Holmes's reply.

Harry sighed. "Merlin once warned me to make sure that the snake I am grasping is not also grasping me."

Harry sat down hard on a chair.

"It rode my vanity!"

"It or someone that knows your patterns, Harry," Holmes added.

Harry gave him a startled look. "Lovecraft!"

Holmes nodded.

"But why would he kill someone that had nothing at all to do with him?"

"Two birds with one stone," Challenger suggested.

Conan glanced at his friend. "I would hardly call Harry and Cherry two birds. They look nothing at all like birds."

Challenger sighed. "Conan, for a doctor, sometimes you're really quite ignorant about practical things."

Ms. Hudson set her knitting down, strode quickly to Harry and gave him a hug around his neck. "Oh Harry, Harry, Harry, don't be so hard on yourself."

He put a hand to her cheek and sighed.

"To think that I might have been the cause of someone's death is terrifying to me," Harry said, his face tight with anger. "Even if not directly."

Ms. Hudson let go, then walked about the table so he could see her face. She wagged a finger at him, then at Holmes. "You two are like mirrors of each other; always carrying the weight of the world on your shoulders."

She said with finality. "You cannot save everyone! You are not God!"

Both Harry and Holmes glanced at each other.

Indeed, they were mirrors for each other.

# Foulinsworth Hall

Harry, Conan, and Challenger scoured the stage of the hall, while Holmes and Watson went through the chairs, one by one, searching for clues.

Holmes stopped once and looked up.

"Is that where he plunged from?" Holmes shouted to Harry, who was picking his way through the box office seats above.

Harry looked to where Holmes was pointing. He shouted back. "Yes."

Holmes nodded, and then continued searching.

Harry paused a moment to wonder why Holmes had asked that question, then it struck him.

Cherry usually perched above the spots, making sure they caught Harry from the start and followed him with every move. Why would he have been near the apron lights?

Harry followed the clue that Holmes had intentionally or unintentionally handed him, his eyes roaming from the apron lights to where the spotlights had been that fatal night.

He froze.

Hurriedly, he ran from the balcony he had stood within and dashed to the fire escape. The escape had a door to the light frame above the stage. Most stagehands preferred climbing the ladders at the side of the stage, but performers preferred the side door. Especially when they had a crucial scene that demanded they set up early and work hard to get everything prepared.

Harry usually helped the stagehands get the lighting the way he wanted it, but what had made Cherry so special, other than his kindly nature and his friendship, was his uncanny and remarkably artistic manner in handling the lights.

Harry always felt like he was being framed for a portrait every time Cherry lit him and the stage about him.

Harry reached the lighting rig hatch door, unlatched it, and then opened it.

"I thought you might have been on to something," Holmes said from behind him.

Harry glanced over his shoulder. Holmes was giving him an encouraging smile.

"It's the most obvious that we often overlook, Harry."

Harry nodded and stepped onto the spider work of beams that carried the lights and provided paths between them. It was set up with a series of crossbeams that were a foot across, with three beams side by side to make a passable walkway that was reasonably safe.

Electrical conduits ran along the side of the beams so that they did not endanger the men walking the crossbeams if they got distracted momentarily, or just were not looking as they should.

Holmes stepped beside Harry and eyed the beams.

Harry pointed to the back beams.

"Cherry usually grabbed me from there and followed me to center stage, then the apron when I needed to step that far."

Holmes eyed the far beams. "It looks pretty safe to me."

"It is. Long as you do not get distracted or careless..."

"Or frightened?" Holmes added.

"That too," Harry agreed.

He turned to Holmes. "If you don't mind, I'd like to check the set up in the back."

"Very well. I'll check the center lighting setup."

They set off in two different directions.

Holmes took the center beams carefully, one step at a time, searching for clues.

Harry reached the back and walked it swiftly. He was very used to the setup here and could have walked it blindfolded and in fact had for one act, where he'd pretended to be blinded by a blown-out light and lost his balance and tumbled to the stage floor, only to not be there at all, but seated in the front row next to the apple vendor.

The audience never could figure that one out, he grinned to himself. But it was one of his lest spectacular tricks. Dummy distracts the audience into believing it is him, while he walks casually to the front row and sits down in the dark of the theater and waits for his fall to the stage.

The dummy strikes the stage.

An explosion of magic.

This is smoke and sparks to hide the fact that the dummy is passing through the stage into the basement below where it is caught by two stagehands, who clean it up for the next performance.

Harry reaches Cherry's lighting position and drops to a knee to examine the lighting setup. The right and left spots are perfectly aligned. They are connected by a swivel bar that allows Cherry to turn them both at the same time in the same direction.

But the center spot seems a bit odd. He leans closer and spots blood on the metal of its frame.

"Holmes!"

"Yes, Harry?"

Harry almost loses his balance. Holmes is standing directly behind him.

"Sorry," Holmes apologizes. He drops to a knee beside Harry and at once spots the blood.

"Interesting," he comments, then rises and begins walking away.

"Aren't you curious why there's blood on the frame, Holmes?"

"Not in the least."

Holmes crosses to the apron beams and then stoops to a knee to examine the lighting rig there. He at once looks over at Harry.

Harry gets up, makes his way around the various curtain riggings, moving a bit recklessly, but more quickly to the spot where Holmes kneels.

Holmes rises, touches the tip of his shoe to a large scorch mark there and spatters of blood about it.

Harry's eyes widen. "It happened here!"

"Indeed, it did, Harry, which would explain how he fell as close to you as to almost strike you."

Harry stood up.

Holmes did as well and investigated Harry's face. "I would say that the man wasn't just murdered..."

"He was used as a bomb to burn me alive as well!" Harry exclaimed unhappily.

He bowed his head unhappily and rubbed at the sudden moistening of his eyes. "Poor Cherry. The man did not deserve to die like this."

"I suspect that once Watson has done the autopsy, we shall find some revealing facts," Holmes announced.

# Scotland Yard Morgue

Harry, Challenger, Conan, and Holmes stand around a large silver metal table on which Cherry's burned body parts are laid out to form his overall shape.

Inspector Bloodstone stands behind Harry, looking over his shoulder.

Constable Evans, the Inspector's son, stands at the door to make sure no one interrupts them.

"This," Watson explained as he touched a gloved finger to the right shoulder blade. "This is where the first trauma struck."

"But why didn't he scream then?" Challenger roared, distraught at the image of the poor man dying so horribly.

Watson gave Challenger a raised eyebrow. "Because the muscle here," he pointed to the striation that looked like smoked meat, "is connected to the neck.

He touched the neck, which just above the muscle was pulled tight.

"It's a rare trick to accomplish murder in this manner, but not impossible," Watson declared as if that settled everything.

"Whatever do you mean, Watson?" Inspector Bloodstone asked.

"Normally, this muscle pulls upon the neck to help it stabilize its position, but in this case the muscle did quite the opposite. It pulled the neck so hard that the blood flow..." He touched another place.

"The Carotid Artery."

"Was blocked!" Conan cried out angrily. "The fiend caused this man to strangle to death!"

Watson nodded. "Yes, he would have felt dizzy at first, but once the blood flow stopped long enough, he would have become brain dead within moments shortly thereafter...his brain starved for oxygen."

Harry clenched his fists. "That explains why he didn't scream, but how did he get from his station to the middle beams if he was dead then?"

"That does appear to be the mystery, doesn't it," Watson agreed.

Holmes eyes narrowed in thought. "I think, Harry, that a trip back to the theater might be in order."

Harry looked at Holmes questioningly.

Holmes, however, was looking at the Inspector. "We will need enough men to guard all entrances and exits from the theater, of course."

The Inspector nodded.

"Of course."

Harry understood at once. "The murderer is still in the theater!" He gasped.

# The Minds of Men

Merlin and Harry stood on the edge of a bluff that overlooked a fast-flowing river below. Butterflies flit back and forth about them.

They stood in a patch of fresh flowering daisies and peonies.

Tiny bees were busily buzzing at their feet as they launched from one flower to the next, gathering pollen to make honey with.

The sun was close to setting and from their advantaged viewpoint, it appeared like a huge bartender with an oversized belly overlapping the bar as he swiped at it with a wet cloth.

The sun was murky looking because of accumulating dust in the air in the distance. While the land was still bright with available light; it was becoming soggier looking as the dust continued to accumulate in the air and swirl about.

"I've never seen a dust devil before, Merlin," Harry said, his eyes taking in the vastness of the nature spirit stirring up the land beneath it.

"Few have, Harry, they are far too busy protecting their hats from blowing off their scalps to see what is grabbing them and hoisting them into the air."

Harry laughed. "Merlin, you know they could not see it anyway. They have not been trained to use their inner vision."

"True enough. Yet, some do not need the training. While others...do. But mostly, the common man lives in a darkened room filled with light and glory and knows little of the vast beauty that exists all about him."

Harry thought about that a moment.

"How can a dark room be filled with light, and one not see?"

Merlin leaned into his staff and cocked his head to look at Harry more closely. His busy eyebrows rolled up and down comically. They were so thick and bushy that they resembled a pair of caterpillars more than hair on his brows.

It is not meant to be taken literally, Harry."

"Then how is it to be taken?" Harry asked.

"With a dash of salt to wake one up and sugar to soothe the nerves once one sees what one has awoken to," Merlin laughed.

Harry grinned.

"So, then you are saying that the average man sees nothing or little of the real world about them?"

"No, I am saying that they choose not to, Harry. And that is the difference between a blind man and a sighted. The one is caught between what he believes and what should be and the other is always stepping past his beliefs to explore territory he has not fully understood yet."

Merlin tapped his staff gently against the ground, sending some bees fluttering off.

"The desire to learn is more powerful in some because they are more developed souls; while the others are yet children in their thoughts."

"I'm lost," Harry sighed.

Merlin grinned. "Not for long."

# Foulinsworth Hall

Holmes watched as the Inspector directed teams of constables to place barriers in front of the entrances in front and several more teams to the sides and back to shut those down as well and guard them.

Constable Evans stood between Harry and Holmes, watching the teams at work.

"Your father is quite expert at this sort of thing, Constable," Holmes noted.

"He's got twenty years on me, so I imagine it's more of a natural thing for him to do these days, though…"

"Yes?"

"Though I sometimes wish he wouldn't try to control everything," Constable Evans finally choked out.

Harry clamped a hand on the constable's shoulder. "My dear fellow, he is a good man and for that you should be glad. Every son eventually wishes to be out from beneath the umbrella of their father and feels stifled. It will pass. And one day your father as well. Be grateful for these times you have with him. They are special."

Holmes gave Harry a look of appreciation. "Well said, Harry."

Constable Evans suddenly made a choking sound, nodded his head, and headed to their right to join with his father.

Harry watched him. "He's such a good kid."

Holmes laughed. "You two are quite close in age as well as wisdom."

"I'm at least four years older," Harry shot back with a grin.

Holmes sighed. "Age has nothing to do with wisdom in the end. In the end it is the willingness to..."

"Open one's heart and mind to the universe and embrace it," Harry finished for him.

Watson came striding quickly up to the two men.

"Challenger and Conan are in place."

"Good," Holmes replied.

He looked at Harry. "You know what to do. We will follow your lead."

"And back you up," Watson added.

Harry smiled at his two friends. "I don't know what I'd do without you two."

"Probably use Challenger and Conan more," Holmes replied with the hint of a smirk.

"But they argue so much," Harry protested.

Holmes smiled at Harry. "One day you will find your better half and understand why," he said, then nodded to Watson, who chuckled lightly, then followed Holmes as he hurried over to speak with the Inspector and the Constable.

# Inside Foulinsworth Hall

Harry spoke softly to his friends, his eyes glancing above to the spider walk above the stage, then back to his friends.

"Conan, I want you and Challenger to stay below the spider walk above. Do not under any circumstance stand directly below it. Do you understand?"

Conan nodded.

Challenger grinned. "The trap door?"

Harry did not grin back. "Some traps are not meant to do what they were constructed for, Challenger. Just obey my instructions."

Challenger lost his grin and nodded.

Conan and Challenger headed down the central aisle, both men nervously glancing about them, even though they did not think there was anything to fear. Yet, something about the air inside the hall was tense, rigid with a kind of sullen, almost angry violence that made both men feel the hair rise on the back of their necks.

Holmes eyed the spider walk above. "Whatever happened, the center was integral to the magic that occurred."

"I agree, Holmes. This kind of magic is very brutal and brutal magic generally uses a different kind of magic to gain its outcome. It is neither parallel nor sympathetic magic. Both those require the subject to have some awareness of it. I doubt that Cherry knew what was happening even when it did."

"Seems reasonable," Holmes agreed, "But let us not forget that it was done in plain sight, during performance hours. So, whomever or whatever performed this act of tragedy not only was not afraid of being exposed but was determined to succeed no matter what."

Holmes waited for Harry to respond.

Harry's face tensed. "Someone who knows me. Knows what I can do if I must. Not someone who followed me."

"Exactly," Holmes replied. "You have been punishing yourself wrongly, Harry. Whatever we finally figure out to be the source of this outrage, I feel certain that it was not your actions that brought it here, but rather its desire to quash your skills."

"Someone who fears competition from me," Harry suggested.

"Or…" Holmes said but did not continue.

Watson and Constable Evans exchanged glances. Constable Evans cleared his throat. Everyone looked at him. "This suspiciously looks like the work of a madman we have been after for some time now."

Harry's face brightened. "Lovecraft!"

Holmes smiled. "I was waiting for that one, Harry. You have become so lost in your grief that your deductive powers were flawed, lessened by your emotions."

"But we considered him before, Holmes," Harry protested.

"But you did not believe it. You felt it was you who had somehow caused Cherry's death, not some sorcerer out for revenge against you. To stop you from stopping his mad quest for domination and control."

"Be wary lest the snake you grasp for, does not grasp you instead!" Harry exclaimed, remembering yet again Merlin's words.

"Of course, it makes perfect sense now; the man needs me out of the way."

"With you out of the way, he feels that Holmes and I would be easy targets," Watson added.

He looked at Holmes. "He's searching for the most vulnerable of us to weaken and destroy and thereby reach us!"

Then Watson grew a horrified look on his face.

"Ms. Hudson!"

# 221B Baker Street

Ms. Hudson sat near the fire, knitting. She did not want to be alone in her flat; too dismal with the weather getting all blustery outside, banging the shutters, blowing loose things against them, and startling her. This was not her favorite time of year.

She hummed happily to herself. She was close to finishing her newest creation, a child's mitten. She had finished the right hand and now she was doing the left. It was for her cousin in France: Cousin Mary.

Her cousin had the most darling daughter.

She smiled.

"MARTHA, WHEN ARE YOU going to have one of these little monsters yourself?" Cousin Mary asked her, her eyes twinkling with mirth as she swung her two-year-old girl in tiny circles, then dropped onto a couch and sat the girl on her lap.

Isabelle, the girl's name, stopped screaming a moment, then kept screaming, reaching her arms up for more.

Cousin Mary jumped to her feet again and swung Isabelle in several more circles.

Ms. Hudson laughed at the joyous occasion. She adored her cousin and Isabelle was the crown jewel of Cousin Mary's life and thus her own as well.

But a part of her felt a certain loss. She wanted a child, but she was not so sure that Watson did. And that made her so sad that she never broached the idea to him. After all they were not married yet. It did not seem proper to weigh him down with the idea of having a baby when he had so much work just keeping up his side of the consulting practice with Holmes all the time.

"Penny for your thoughts, Martha!" Cousin Mary announced, placing Isabelle into Ms. Hudson's arms.

Ms. Hudson rose from her chair and rubbed her nose against that of Isabelle, who giggled and rubbed at her nose afterwards. "Tickles!" She cried out, laughing very sweetly.

BANG!

Cousin Mary looked at Ms. Hudson. "What was that?"

BANG! BANG!

BANG!

Ms. Hudson spilled her knitting to the floor and jumped from her chair, alarmed at the sound. What was it? It sounded like it had come from downstairs.

BANG!

Then she knew from where.

Her flat!

Oh my God! She suddenly remembered she had left a window open and unshuttered.

She fled down the stairs, thinking it was merely the wind playing with the shudder.

She flung open her door.

Something stood in the shadowy depths of her sitting room. Something large!

Ms. Hudson at once flung the door shut and ran back up the stairs. She shut that door as well. She put her back to it, her heart racing. What was it she had seen?

Then she heard the sounds.

Footsteps.

Heavy.

Heavy footsteps.

Climbing the stairs.

"John!" She uttered, barely above a whisper. "I need you!" She cried out in a choking voice.

Something heavy struck the door at her back.

# Trap

Harry and Merlin were kicking at the dandelions on the path they followed through the woods, sending small clouds of their delicate floating seeds into the air.

"This is so much fun!" Harry laughed.

Merlin smiled and chuckled. "Simple pleasures are always the best."

Having run out of dandelions to kick into the air, they finally stopped at a large boulder that sat at the edge of a small rushing creek. Its burbling waters smashed against stone and shore, making a sound that was very pleasing. Very soothing to the senses.

Harry kicked off his shoes at once, sat down on the bank and dangled his toes in the water.

"Bait!" Merlin exclaimed.

Harry at once withdrew his toes, not sure whether that was a warning or not.

Merlin laughed. "No, Harry, not your toes, the allure of something soothing."

Merlin sat next to him and cupped a handful of the flowing water, drank it slowly, his face relaxed and peaceful. Finished he wiped his beard and mustache with the back of his hand, and then sat back, leaning on his staff to watch the occasional leaf scooting past on the water, a tiny beetle riding its back like a human in a sailboat headed to sea.

"Nature is always full of surprises," Merlin commented.

Harry, finally feeling safe again, put his toes back into the water."

"Bait!" Exclaimed Merlin.

Harry at once plucked his toes back out again.

"Merlin!" He complained.

Merlin laughed. "Not your toes this time either. It is the sense of complacency that drives us sometimes into making a mistake we might not otherwise perform."

Harry did not stick his toes back into the water, even though he wanted to...very badly!

"Is there a point to this, Merlin?"

Merlin sighed. "There is a point to everything we do in life Harry. Our life is our book. What is written in it, is what we live, what we do, what we breathe."

"What we learn from?" Harry added hopefully.

Merlin fixed a smile on Harry and ruffled his thick hair with his left hand. "Indeed, Harry. Indeed!"

# Shudders

A police wagon pulled next to the curb and stopped.

Watson, Harry, Holmes got out of the backseat of Constable Evan's police wagon and Conan and Challenger from the rear. They dropped lightly to the pavement and then froze.

The window to Ms. Hudson's flat was open, the shudders shattered.

"Martha!" Cried Watson and rushed for the front door.

# 221B Baker Street

Ms. Hudson looked about the sitting room desperately. There must be something she could use to protect herself. She asked herself.

She hurriedly went through the room.

Nothing!

Then she noticed the large poker by the fireplace. She grabbed it and hefted it over her shoulder and turned to face the door.

BANG!

The wood began to splinter at the hinges.

BANG!

The door smashed inwards.

Something straight from hell entered.

She took one look at it and began backing up. It was hideous. Taller than Holmes. Its skin was yellowish with green scars that exuded a kind of slime that crawled about the scars, making it seem more like a slug than human.

It had human shaped hands, but its fingers were tentacles. Its head was a huge bubble with floating eyes that rotated about it. Many, many eyes.

She did not scream.

She was not that kind of woman.

She also did not try to run away to her credit. It was more than likely to go after her. And there was nowhere else to hide. If it could break down the front door and now this one, there no other would stop it.

She faced it squarely raising her poker higher.

"Whatever you are, I'm not scared of you," she told it.

Inwardly, she was shaking with terror.

It hissed at her, and a tongue shot out like a lizard's tongue, coming to within several inches of her face, where it seemed to float for a long time with an eye sprouting from its tip to gaze at her.

BLAM!

A terrible roar.

The creature jerked hard, startled by the sound, but untouched by the bullet that had struck the hallway wall.

"MARTHA!' Watson shouted.

She did not have time to respond. The creature rushed her, opening its jaws wide as it did so.

She swung with all her might at its face.

The poker sank all the way into its flesh. At least half a dozen of its eyes burst, scattering a green and

yellow ichor over her and the floor.

The creature let out a second terrible roar and reached up to grasp the poker and pull it free. It then gave her a hideous smile. The smile of death!

She backed up against the wall. There was nowhere else to flee to.

BLAM! BLAM! BLAM!

Three gunshots.

The hideous creature turned about to face Holmes, Watson and Constable Evans who had their weapons out, their barrels smoking.

"Martha!" Watson cried out, his face crazy with worry for her life.

He tried to dart for her, but Homes and Constable Evans restrained him.

Then Harry stepped into the room just as the monster swung its head about again to go after Ms. Hudson.

"I think not!" Harry announced tensely.

The creature turned about to look at who had spoken. Its eyes widened and then it gave Harry a hideous smile.

"Eat!" It said with a sound that made the skin crawl on everyone in the room.

Harry stepped in front of the others. "Martha, it is not you it really wants. It is me! Go into Holmes room and lock the door. Now!"

Ms. Hudson ran for the hallway and into Holmes room and locked it.

Harry stepped in front of his friends, his right fist behind his back.

"You know you have gone too far this time. You hurt a man very dear to me and now you try to harm a woman who is the light of my life and that of my best friend's. This creature shall not pass, Lovecraft!"

The creature launched its tongue at Harry.

Holmes and Watson fired their weapons. The tongue exploded in a shower of putrescent flesh and ichor.

Harry smiled as he stepped closer to the creature, which howled in pain and sucked in what was left of its tongue.

"Lovecraft, I know you are behind this, and I shall find you!" Harry promised.

Then he whipped his right hand from behind his back as the monster rushed him. A flood of pure blue energies shot forth and enveloped the monster in a burning rage of blue searing light.

Harry, Holmes, and Watson clapped hands over their ears. The scream of the monster was so loud that it shattered the windowpanes and every piece of glass within the flat.

Harry staggered a moment. He had been the closest to the sonic blow, and then he steadied.

He aimed his fist again and this time fired even more energy at the creature, who had been working free of the cocoon of blue forces wrapped about it. The creature spun about and staggered with its back to the shattered window frames.

Harry then ran at the creature and flew into the air, landing a right foot square in its chest.

The creature flew backwards, smashed through what remained of the sitting room windows and tumbled outside.

The sound of screeching tires outside, then more gunshots.

# Death Stroke

Harry and Holmes rushed outside, where they found the smoldering body of the monster lying on the pavement.

A traffic jam was piling up as citizens got out looking at the remains of the monster.

Conan and Challenger stood five feet away, with weapons out.

Challenger's long gun pointed at the remains.

"Harry, you did a right fancy job on whatever this thing was but my trusty Betty here..."

Challenger kissed the barrel of his long gun. "...It helped put the finishing touches on this nasty work of art."

Challenger turned away and headed for the steps. "Always have hated abstract art," he muttered as he climbed the stairs.

Harry stood over the remains. "Holmes, better see to Ms. Hudson and Watson," he told him. "I'll finish up here."

Holmes nodded and headed back up the stairs.

Conan joined Harry. "Right messy sort of thing whatever it was."

Harry suddenly looked up.

His right fist blazed.

"And I know from where it came!"

Harry jerked the wand from his belt and pounded across the street to the opposing building, where he blasted the front door open with a searing red explosion of fire and smoke, then burst inside and out of view.

Conan followed him, though a bit more cautiously because of the fire that was now blazing about the frame of the door.

# 221B Baker Street

"Magic is a double-edged sword," Harry explained as he sipped at a cup of tea. His clothing was burnt, and his hair singed in places. His skin was filthy from ash and burnt paint flakes.

He looked even worse now than he had earlier prior to their return to the hall and then back to save Ms. Hudson.

Conan was not in much better shape, but he was smiling as he listened.

Challenger sat by the fire cleaning his long gun, just listening.

Ms. Hudson and Watson cuddled near the hallway their chairs turned towards the shattered windows where two men in uniform were busily working to repair the frame.

Constable Evans came up the stairs with a silver plate of sandwiches which he sat on the table.

"Oh, Constable, you're such a dear!" Ms. Hudson complimented him; her face lit up with a smile.

Constable Evans touched his cap. "Least I could do for my friends," he said, his eyes not leaving hers.

She dimpled and gave her attention back to Watson, who said. "I will never leave you alone again. I swear it!"

She lightly slapped his right hand. "John, you will do no such thing. I am a big girl now and I can take care of myself."

Harry held his right fist out and clenched it so tight that the knuckles began making crackling sounds, and then he opened it. A tiny necklace, with a softly glowing blue stone at its throat lay there.

"I want you to have this, Martha," he told her.

Ms. Hudson took it into her hands. "It's beautiful."

"It's so much more than that," Harry said, leaning towards her. "I agree with Watson. You must never be left alone again. Least until we have caught this Lovecraft character and put him out of business."

"You mean blow his brains out don't you, Harry?" Challenger remarked casually.

Harry glared at Challenger. "Need we be so crude in speaking of it?"

Challenger laughed but did not say Harry was right either.

"But why the necklace, Harry?" Ms. Hudson asked, as she slipped it about her neck.

Harry smiled. "It is connected to me. Everything you feel I will feel..."

"Say now..." Watson growled, rising to scowl at Harry.

Harry chuckled. "Not those kinds of feelings, Watson. Merely the ones that do not belong there."

Watson gave Harry a look of disbelief and doubt but said no more and sat down again next to Ms. Hudson, who was laughing her head off.

She reached over to him and gave him a sweet kiss on his cheek. "My dear, dear grumbly bear!"

"I am not..."

He broke into a grin and gave Harry a look of embarrassment. "Sorry, Harry."

"Apology accepted," Harry replied with a grin of his own.

Holmes sipped at his coffee a moment, and then said, "It's funny that he's been right across the street all this time..."

"...And we didn't know it," Watson finished for him.

Ms. Hudson shuddered. "I did. I have been getting these cold flashes every time I left our flat and went outside."

Watson put an arm about her shoulders and pulled her tightly against him. "I'm sorry you had to go through that."

She laughed. "With you gentlemen, a lady never has a dull moment, you know. And some of us girls are not afraid of a bit of rough and tumble now and then."

They broke into laughter.

Conan spoke up, his mustache crinkling comically as he did so, "Where do you think he went?"

Harry sighed. "The simulacrum he sent after Ms. Hudson had to have been at least a day old or it would have perished. They cannot last more than twenty-four hours."

"Simulacrum?" Challenger asked.

"It is sort of like that Golem thing in literature. But made from rotting flesh, instead of clay."

"Yuck!" Conan spit out. "Only thing I hate more than slimy flesh is rotting flesh."

Holmes grinned at Conan. "And this from a doctor, hey, Conan?"

Conan gave Homes a hurt look. "I'm still a man, Holmes, even if one of the best doctors and writers there has ever been..." he added with a smirk. "And I have you to prove that!" He said with finality, glaring at Challenger to contradict him.

Challenger merely smiled.

Everyone burst into laughter.

The constables working on the windows finished, drew the shades across them and touched their caps to Constable Evans.

"Done, Constable," the taller one said.

Constable Evans rose, setting down his coffee cup. "I'll give the two of you a ride home, unless that is, you'd like to stop for a mug of ale beforehand?" He asked in a sly voice.

The two constables gave him a happy smile and nodded vigorously.

Constable Evans turned to Ms. Hudson. "I am so grateful you weren't harmed, Ms. Hudson. I know it would have broken my father's heart as well as mine, had it been so."

Ms. Hudson broke away from Watson, stood up, then came to Constable Evans and gave him a warm hug

"You are a good man, Constable Evans. Some day you are going to make a fine husband and father as well."

He laughed. "I'd settle for just a happy constable for the moment, if you please!"

She laughed and he turned to his fellow officers, nodded and they exited the room.

She sat back down next to Watson, who put his arm about her shoulders again.

"John, there's something we need to talk about," she said, with a vision of a bouncing baby girl growing increasingly clear in her mind.

He gave her an inquisitive look.

Holmes turned to his friends. "What say we go to the pub down the street?"

Challenger, Conan, and Harry all rose and followed Holmes to the coat rack, put on their coats and hats and tramped down the stairs and out of view, their laughing voices loud at first as they left and then fading after they shut the replaced front door.

Watson looked at Ms. Hudson, his face confused. "I can't understand what has possibly gotten into all of them to leave so suddenly," he told her.

She smiled.

She knew why.

And then she told him why.

"Oh!" Was his only word afterwards.

# THE THIRD TRANSFORMATION

# Transformation

*S*ome years back.

"Ladies and Gentlemen," Harry announced to the gathered audience in the Globe Theater, all of whom whose eyes were now frozen on his semi naked figure, which while not perfect, was evenly muscled and firmly packed with strength.

Harry ran every day early in the morning up and down the stairs of Scotland Yard, where constables would smile and greet him and then he would take a lap about the building, even passing arriving criminals being herded into the back area, where they would be booked and herded into awaiting cells.

So, he was not out of shape.

He even spent an hour each day, usually before bed, as it helped him to relax, lifting weights. How? He would donate his time to the local Home for the Elderly, where he would lug the heavy crates of donated food up and down the five flights of stairs from the basement to the kitchen area.

Everyone there knew him, because he always performed a magic show for the older ones every holiday and arrived on Christmas morning to hand out unique gifts, he made himself. He loved to carve fresh wood into mythological creatures.

Each gift he handed out he would give a short story about the creature and its history.

But this night he was not doing that, he was preparing to launch himself headfirst into a flaming tank of burning oil and water.

He had never performed this trick before.

It was risky because if he remained in the water too long, the heat from the burning oil would soon boil him along with the water and if he did not break free from the cuffs locking his hands behind his back, he would surely die of suffocation and drown if the boiling water had not already finished him first.

So, he was motivated to do well.

Highly motivated.

Harry continued, "Tonight I shall perform the most horrific and dangerous magic stunt I have ever created. I call it the Burning Boiling Doom!"

Everyone gasped in the theater.

Only the rustling of mugs of mead, hot potatoes being crunched between lips and the sucking in of breath by those fearful for him could be heard.

Some of the ladies in front were very openly dangling their handkerchiefs in a certain way to gain his attention, hoping that after the show, he would find them and with their handkerchief return to them that which they wanted, which was not the cloth, but his affection.

Harry, still being young and hormonally driven at times, would sometimes take them up on their offers. Even as he had the night before, which explained why he did not feel his normal bright eyed, bushy tailed self this evening.

He saw one fall and nodded to the damsel. It was Mina, the love of his life and the bane of his life. He had never loved a woman so terribly strong and at the same time been so horribly conflicted in his feelings.

Loving a vampire is not easy, especially when their father is the King of Vampires, Count Dracula. But so far, they had kept their tryst a secret from him. He dreaded what would happen if they did not. He had this terrible fear of fang sinking into his throat and sucking his life away.

He had no reason to bring dishonor to the Count. So far, they only spent hours together talking. Always talking and talking. And for a young man like himself, with so many opportunities to not...talk, it was a rare and precious thing indeed.

Without further word, he glanced across his vast theater filled audience, nodded to William Shakespeare who sat in the top balcony with the Good Queen Mary of Scots, and then began climbing to the top of the large cylindrical bottle he would become immersed in. Once upside down, the only way out was for him to uncuff himself, twist about and fly to the surface and hurl him out onto the platform to save him.

He smiled. Let them think that. He had other plans. Then he lost his arrogant smile. If they worked.

He waited until the house constable, a young man with flaming red hair and a mischievous twinkle to his eyes latched the cuffs onto his wrists behind his back.

"Thank you, Constable Evans," he said.

Constable Evans nodded. "God's luck to you, Harry."

"Oh, I'll need that and more," Harry snorted with a smile on his lips.

Constable Evans stepped back and crossed his arms to wait for Harry to escape into his arms.

They were both to be disappointed.

Harry descended headfirst into the cylinder of water. It was cold. He had requested that to offset the initial heat of the burning oil on top.

An assistant dressed in the appropriately excited costume of brilliant reds and golds stepped forward with a lit torch.

Constable Evans nodded to her. She smiled at him.

They had a dinner afterwards.

Then she turned and flung the torch into the water.

Immediately it flared to life as the oil caught fire.

The audience gasped in fear.

The tension had started to build.

The assistant turned to the audience. "Mister Houdini will have but two minutes to escape the Burning Boiling Doom or perish!"

Gentleman up and down the aisles and in the booths above took out pocket watches to time the seconds and minutes, glancing at Harry as he hung upside down in the water.

The assistant announced. "The cuffs that the good Constable Evans has placed on Mister Houdini have no key for them. They cannot be unlocked by any pick or piece of metal known to man."

Constable Evans nodded to her after glancing at his watch.

"Sixty seconds left! The assistant announced.

# Awakening of Magic

O f rain and shine
	Morning and night
Wet and Cold
Hot and soothing,
The world is not awry
A slide into confusion.
It is a course of wonders
That thunders through us.
—John Watson
*Many years back.*
It was a dark and dreary night.

Isn't it usually when everything you planned goes completely awry?

Slices of sizzling bolts of electricity arced across the skies and struck the earth, gouging and pounding it like a butcher tenderizing meat to be eaten. Except that for Harry, it was his body that was threatened to become meat.

He ran as fast as his youthful feet would carry him through the Golden Woods, ignoring the faces buried in the overhanging canopies of leaves and moss from the thickly clustered trees that carved themselves into the hillside he ran about. Crunching wood beneath his feet startled him because he was not expecting it and he almost fell when the fallen bark turned into fallen branches of larger and large sizes that stuck, prodded, and poked at him, grasping for his ankles and legs in attempts to hold him back and slow him down.

But he was not going to be discouraged by the constant challenges. He was not one to give up easily, or to shirk difficulties that might arise. He had learned from early on that anything tough enough to defeat you was also challenge enough to strive and overcome.

He recovered his balance, stifled a threatening sob, and clutching his rains slicked fists continued to pound towards his goal. A cave.

And not just any cave.

The fabled Crystal Caves of Merlin.

Fabled, because none had found them prior to his accidental discovery; and fabled because even though Merlin was still a strong presence in the new Britains, he was still considered a thing of magic, and even though magic was rising once more in the realms, it was feared greatly because of the consequent parallel growth of evil.

Slam!

A bolt of lightning struck a huge boulder that loomed out of the darkness to his right. Splinters of stone sliced through the leaf canopy, and one struck his right ear. He immediately cried out in pain and once more almost fell, but recovered, with a hand grabbing a bush next to him to right himself.

But as he grabbed it, he felt something move across his knuckles. He glanced that way and saw the nose of a bear.

He screamed.

The bear screamed.

Harry dashed away, driven by the force of terror as well as fear now.

But nothing pursued him.

No monster.

And certainly, no bear. It was smart enough to stay out of the rain, thunder and slicing bolts of lightning that ached to carve the unwary traveler into smoking heaps of burnt flesh.

Harry was not yet wise nor old enough to realize that it was only men you had to fear, that nature was never out to deliberately get you...to strike you down...to maim, rape or torture you as men have done through the ages and continue to do, much to the dismay of those they trespass.

"Butt up, Harry!" He whispered to himself as he continued his curve about the hill, showing yet again that though no old, nor necessarily that wise yet, still he was clever enough, smart enough to know what he wanted and to not give up.

Whenever things got tough, his father would slam his hand against Harry's bottom, not as hard as to hurt dreadfully, but enough to alert him to pay attention.

"Butt up, Harry! Life's your friend not your enemy!"

As Harry ran like the devil was after him, he remembered those words repeatedly. Because he was trying to keep up his morale. When he had begun the hike to the cave this morning, he had not realized how far the cave was. He wished now he had never searched through his uncle's memoirs, then he would not be so foolishly dashing through a night of storm and thunder, lightning and God only knew what else yet remained in his path.

But as all nights of terror begin, they also must end.

Several yards ahead of Harry several bolts of lightning cut across the rain drenched skies and revealed a huge dark blot between several larger trees.

# Transformation 2

*S*ome *years back.*

    Harry could feel the heat of the boiling water above him stretching out to grasp his ankles and feet. At this point it was no more than a brisk bath might be, but he knew in a matter of fifteen second or more, the heat would reach his chest and then his heart would begin to boil within it.

He would die.

He felt the solidity of the cuffs behind him. Carefully, he probed the locking mechanism from the outside, feeling its length, breadth, and depth with his fingers.

While the lock had no known key, it did have a mechanism to close and latch it. He had learned of this torture device from a Chinese scholar who described it as a favorite way that the Dark Wizards there used to torture victims. Promising freedom if they could release themselves in a certain amount of time.

They never did.

But Harry was not them. He was young, optimistic and quite, quite clever.

Fourteen seconds left he told himself, feeling his lungs start to burn from holding his breath.

He continued to play with the lock, giving his audience as good a show as possible, but not so much that he would die. He had no intentions of meeting the good people on the other side of the Path of Light just yet.

The assistant above glanced at Constable Evans. He held up ten fingers two times.

She turned to the audience, who could see Harry now begin to squirm as if he were unable to free himself. His movements got more intense and worrisome.

Shakespeare's confection attendants sold everything they carried inside the theater and more as the theater goers ate voraciously to calm their agitated nerves and growing fear for Harry's life.

Constable Evans held up just ten fingers.

"Harry has only ten seconds of breath left," she announced. "And no more than five after that before he boils to death!" She announced in a fatal tone.

Constable Evans smiled back at her when she winked at him, but he was also getting worried. Harry had told him he would have the cuffs off sooner than this. But he waited patiently. Harry had given him strict orders.

But as he thought that he glanced at the audience and saw a dark faced man standing there with a pair of handcuffs exactly like those of Harry's. The man gave Constable Evans a smile that made him think of only one thing: Harry had been tricked!

# The Crystal Caves of Merlin

P ut your dreams
	Where they belong
In hope
And in song
Leave the real work
Of living
Where it belongs.
—Merlin

*Many years back.*

Harry burst through the several bushes that overhung and sided the cave opening, making the last several feet with a magnificent leap...of faith and strength.

For he did not know at all what he was leaping into, only that he must.

Do not ask him now why, or then why, he just knew he must.

And several seconds later a huge bolt of lightning struck the path where he would have stood had he not made his last leap. The ground was torn up and exploded upwards, leaving a smoking crater.

Harry was cast to the rocky floor of the cave, his thick cotton shirt wet from rain and now smoking from the sudden flare of heat.

He remembered what his father had told him about fire and quickly rolled over and over until it was smothered. But when he sat up, his shoulder ached. He reached back and could tell that his long hair in the back was crisped by the blast of flames. Even the back of his neck was slightly burned.

Later, when he returned home, his father would do the butt warning again, but much harder and then he and his mother would both hug him, sobbing with relief that he was alive, having feared the storm had taken him away from them.

But for now, his thoughts were only on the sudden pain and discomfort of his body.

"Pain is just a thought, Harry," a voice whispered.

Harry staggered to his feet, still feeling weak and woozy from the fall and the blast. His ears rung from the intensity of it. But he knew what he must do.

He reached into his right pants pocket and took out a small leather pouch with matches in it. He took one out and struck it on the rough wall of the cave entrance.

It lit so brightly, he winced for a moment against it, and then turned slowly to reveal the cave better. And as he did, he spotted an antique lantern hanging on a carved hanger on the wall to the right of the entrance.

The lantern was one of those old kinds that have no glass and is carried like a bowl of soup. He went to it, but it was out of reach.

After all, he was only ten. And ten is still small for most boys and he was probably never going to be tall, as his father anyway. At least that is what he thought then, even if later it was to be proved otherwise.

He scouted the floor a bit and spotted a large rock. He yelped. The match had burned to his fingers. He tossed it away, the crouched to move the rock. It was very heavy, but by putting his back into it, he was able to gradually move it to the foot of the wall where the lantern hung.

He climbed onto the rock. It wobbled a bit from his weight but held. He reached up and was barely able to grasp the lantern.

It took him several long moments of tugging to remove it from its stone hanger, but he finally did and got a face full of some coarse liquid as reward.

It dribbled into his mouth, and he said, "Yuck!"

It tasted foul.

Then he realized what it was before he tossed the lantern away. It was not water, but oil. A thick one, truly, but serviceable to his needs.

He climbed down from the rock, set the lantern on top of it, and then fumbled into his pants again for the leather pouch of matches. He thanked God that he had the foresight to use a leather pouch, or they would surely have been so drenched by now that they would not ignite, let alone burn steadily.

He struck a match against the cave wall and then lowered it towards the thick lantern oils. Amid them he spotted something dark. He used his other hand to plunge into the oil and found a thick wick. He pulled it from beneath the oil and then put the match to it.

The wick caught fire and burned fiercely a moment, almost blinding him, then settled to a pleasant steady burn.

"Well then," he uttered, absolutely pleased with himself.

Another thing he remembered at that moment was his father telling him, "You are special, Harry. You are not like the other children. God has plans for you."

At the time he frowned. Who was this God thing that his father kept bringing up? But now he knew his father was just showing him fatherly love and respect. Encouraging him.

How did he know that?

Because it is exactly what he did with his best friend, Challenger, an older kid, monstrously tall for his years. He was fiercely freckled and had long curly even more fierce hair that always got in his face and nostrils.

He was funny and bright at the same time.

He was the one who got Harry onto the tracks of the caves he was now in.

"Harry, kiddo," Challenger had told him with that roguish grin of his, "You want to do magic; you gotta go to its source!"

Even in those days Challenger was preparing to be the explorer he would become...the great adventurer who would one day bring a living dinosaur to London and almost get himself killed in the process.

# Transformation Three

*S ome years back.*

Harry suddenly realized the cuffs were not the ones that Constable Evans had originally planned to use on him. The mechanism was unforgiving and somehow unrelenting. It would not budge.

He looked out; his face suddenly filled with terror.

The audience outside saw and gasped, rising to their feet as they thought he was about to boil to death and drown.

Harry shut his eyes and forced himself to relax. As he did so, he saw his mentor in his mind.

The man leaned on his tall staff and smiled at Harry.

"No door is shut, Harry, that you cannot find another to open," the man had told him.

Constable Evans flew down the platform stairs and ran screaming to the side stage. "An axe. Quickly an axe!"

He had to break Harry free before he was drowned or boiled. He had only a few seconds to do so.

A brilliant flare of light erupted behind him, causing the audience to gasp.

The man who had tricked Harry frowned and then fled the theater.

The great glass cylinder tipped over and spilled Harry and the flaming water across the stage.

Harry flopped over like a floundering fish, and then said in Latin, "Finis!"

The flames that were threatening to spread to the platform and to the audience in front flared a brilliant blue and vanished.

The water froze.

Harry slowly stood up and raised his hands over his back, the cuffs falling away to the floor.

He smiled triumphantly as what few of the audience who were yet seated jumped to their feet and erupted into a thunderous applause.

Constable Evans ran back with the axe and slid on the ice.

The audience gasped as Harry was now threatened by the out-of-control Constable with the axe in his hands.

At the last possible moment Constable Evans flung his axe safely aside and fell into Harry's outstretched arms.

Harry smiled into the startled constable's face. "We really got to stop meeting this way, Constable," he announced loudly.

This time Harry and Constable Evans were buried n flowers, candies, and handkerchiefs, from men and women as thunderous applause shook the very foundations of the Globe Theater.

Shakespeare ran up to the stage, clapping the entire way. He leaped onto the stage from the side stairs onto the apron, skirted the frozen water, grabbed Harry's right arm, and raised it up high in the air.

Harry winced. When he had contorted to free the cuffs at the last possible moment, he had to dislocate that shoulder and it still hurt from doing so.

"I give you Harry Houdini, Master Magician..."

The crowd went crazy again.

".... And..." Shakespeare continued. "...the greatest living Wizard since Merlin the Magician."

Harry was stunned.

Even the audience was stunned.

They all turned their heads upwards to see what Good Queen Mary of Scots thought of that announcement.

They did not have long to think about it. She rose elegantly put her hands out over the balcony and began clapping long and loudly.

Harry's fame had now been firmly proven.

But despite all that had happened to his benefit, as Merlin might have said, there was a thorn yet to be revealed.

The dark man who had tricked Constable Evans and...him!

He glanced about the theater, the man was long gone, but something inside of Harry, maybe his fear, maybe his intuition, told him he hadn't seen the last of that blaggart!

And then Shakespeare repeated what he said earlier, jarring Harry back to the present.

"I give you Master Magician, Harry Houdini, the greatest magician in the world!"

Harry smirked. Now that was pushing things a bit he thought, but allowed Shakespeare his words, because it was good for his business, and at this moment Harry only wanted the night to be over with.

He glanced over at Mina, who gave him an alluring smile.

Yes, he was ready to have the night over.

He smiled back, already thinking of the wonderful time they would be spending together after the show.

Then he frowned.

But if only it could always be that way.

Show business was...well, showing off. And even if he could not personally get behind it, he had a business manager he loved and a great staff that worked magic in their own personal ways to help him do his work on stage and create a profit for all of them.

Sometimes, he thought it a bit excessive...his wealth and fame. Yet, when he considered how many impoverished people, he was able to anonymously help through their struggles, the charities he helped and encouraged, perhaps God's Grace unto him was not as excessive as he sometimes...when in overwhelm or exhaustion...felt to be the case.

So, Harry did what was expected of him, he took the praise and bowed repeatedly as the applause and roar of "Here, Here," thundered throughout the Globe Theater.

When it began to lighten, he did an extraordinary thing. And probably the thing that had driven Mina away from him for years.

He spoke up.

Loudly.

"Drinks are on me!" He shouted.

And they were.

One after the other.

Even as his assistants cleaned up the mess on stage, Shakespeare happily joined the growing crowd of men and women who stayed after the show to celebrate with Harry.

He had thought Mina would join him, but as she left, she had turned back, and he could see nothing but disappointment on her face.

And that had been the last he had seen of her for years.

Maybe if he had done something different, he would never have become what he was this day...a wizard of power and a showman of extraordinary talent. He never thought of himself in terms of great or wonderful, even when his billings for his shows were plastered all over the place with such heady and gaudy reminders to the public. And yet, he was billed as such. So perhaps there was some truth to it, even though his humility never allowed him the peace of mind to believe otherwise.

But tonight, even though he had managed to outshine all expectations of him.

He had become a hero.

Even so.

At this moment Harry felt a great sadness begin to edge over his heart. Perhaps fame was not worth so much if it meant losing the dearest part of your soul.

"Mina," he whispered to no one.

"Harry Houdini," a young woman's voice jerked him from his reverie.

She came up so close to him that her large bosom brushed his chest. There was no shame in her eyes.

Maybe, had Mina stayed? No certainly, if she had stayed, things would have turned in a different direction, but she did not.

He looked into the young woman's eyes. "You're the one who dropped the pink handkerchief."

She looked down at her feet.

There it was now over his feet.

He smiled.

Perhaps this night wasn't a total loss, he thought to himself as he stooped to retrieve it and hand it to her.

Her smile promised him many things as she retrieved it from his hand, taking hold of it and his hand at the same time. "I hear the stars are quite beautiful from Astoria Park this time of night."

Astoria Park was near his home.

She gave him a slight nudge with her bosom, and he felt a rush of excitement.

"Would you care for a walk?" He asked, reaching his arm out.

"Most certainly."

Then he laughed. He was still half naked.

"After I dress, of course."

"I'd like nothing better," she said, leaving him no doubt as to what she meant or what her intentions were.

# Discovery

M*any years back.*

Despite all the trepidation, fear, and memories of discouragement, or more likely in Harry's case, because of them...he went ahead to explore the unknown the dark depths of the cave he had wanted to explore: Merlin's Crystal Caves.

Legendary thought they were, they were still of the earth and thus lots of dirt, stone and other things that walked, whisked, flew, and clung.

He swept aside a large veil of spider moss, which grows from the ceiling down and is more like a tapestry than actual moss, even though it is quite spongy to the touch and when it gets moist from water, a bit slimy.

Getting past his initial disgust with the touch of the spider moss, he shoved it aside and stepped past the living tapestry and allowed it to fall behind him.

If it was dark before; it was now almost pitch black. Even Harry's incredible night vision was challenged by this.

The entrance to the cave, though well hidden, could never describe in any depth what was inside. While seemingly old, moldy, and cramped at first, as he walked more into it and the cave opened wider and wider, the magnificence of it began to hammer into his fears and wipe them away, like water washing dirt from a plate. Even with so much shadowy and hard to see in detail, he could see enough to feel like he had just walked from the earthy realms into that of Fairie, a world of beings who Merlin had caused to separate from mankind for the protection, not of mankind, but of Fairie.

While man was maturing as a species, he still, for the most part remained greedy and aggressive, and murdering when it came to treasure.

All these thoughts and more passed through Harry's mind as he ducked and dodged, slipped and climbed along the path, wary of sharp stones and slithering things, of which there were many...scorpions, hammerhead beetles, snails with magnificent eye stalks that glowed in the dark, as well as the usual suspects...bats that heard him coming and hated the disturbance so flung themselves at him, missing him by fractions of an inch as they passed overhead, making high pitched screaming sounds.

Even as a child he had to be careful not to strike his head on overhanging rocks, but he managed to get inside, deeper, and deeper. And the further he went the more awestruck he was.

Merlin had left markers along the way, evidently because some of the cave was quite dangerous. He knew that because he ignored the first marker and ended up at a dead end, but the second marker he avoided brought him to a sudden pitfall, which he started to tumble into, but only his quick reflexes and more than a ton of luck saved him from.

He had clung to the edge of the drop off, his right hand clutching the hard ridged edge, cutting into his palm painfully and truly regretting not trusting his intuition and the markers.

That had been a big lesson for him from day one, trust your intuition!

He had found his second handhold, then a foothold, but barely. He regained a foothold, but his hand slipped. He quickly slung his other hand up and caught hold, but at the price of cutting his other hand deeply. Harry could feel blood oozing along his wrist as he pulled himself upwards. That and something else!

That several feet he had dropped was covered with a living wall of insects. Slimy, nauseous insects.

Slugs!

*I hate slugs*, Harry thought to himself.

But he did not let go. He hated death even more.

His nose and mouth scraped the disgusting things and several times some of them latched onto his face and began crawling up it.

*Ewwww!*

He had to spit one out that was trying to crawl into his mouth and blow hard with both nostrils when one tried to enter his nasal passage.

But finally, after long painful seconds he had his first leg, then his second over the lip of the drop off. He would have lain there to recover his wits, but more of the slugs were crawling on his hands and several started to enter his gaping mouth as he gasped for air.

*Ewwww* twice as much!

Harry scrambled to his feet and hurriedly brushed off the other slugs on him.

Then he saw that the lantern was standing upright, just half its fluid gone. A miracle it had not spilled out.

That worried him, not the miracle, but the fact that half the liquid was gone. He had used almost half to get this far. He did not think he had enough to go further, let alone return.

He was not so sure how long it would last, but his curiosity finally got the better of him.

So here he was at a branch of the caves, and a clear marker to the right that glows a luminescent green. And that would have been it, but there was also a marker on his left, also luminescent and bright, but a deep violent red that kept swirling with seeming menace.

*Now what?* He thought.

That is when he saw the writing in Latin on the wall in front of him. He held his lantern closer and read it aloud.

"Here be a choice for the man with little or no voice; choose the path you will follow or fall into a sleepy hollow in death's lost repose."

What?

"Red is the passion for life of a man driven and green is the path less given. Make your choice and make it wise. For here becomes a man or one who is wise."

Ewwwww. He thought again. Except it were not slugs this time, but rhymes. And not just funny or melodious rhymes, but choices.

If he went further one of two things could happen.

Judging from his first mistake he felt intuitively that it could be fatal to make the wrong one, so he sat down and pondered the meaning of the words.

Then his lantern began to flicker frantically. "Oh no!" He cried out.

Then the lantern went dark.

Ewwwww!

# What Path Lies Ahead?

*Many years back.*

He woke up with the back of his head aching, as well as his back and legs, which he had crossed over in his sitting position. Something he had learned from a Hindu his father knew. Was supposed to increase blood flow and relaxation.

He did not know about the blood part of it, but he had just fallen asleep. So, the relaxation part worked.

He felt about him and then remembered where he was. His hand discovered the extinguished lantern. He felt for the wall behind him and then slowly rose, using it to steady him.

He was not afraid of the dark. Had he been, he would never have made this journey from the beginning. But now he was not only in the dark, but in an extremely dangerous series of caves, where one misstep could lead to certain death.

Why would Merlin live in such a place? Or more importantly, why would he leave it so dangerous?

Harry then saw the two glowing markers, but the words on the wall had changed.

"Choose the right path to freedom, the wrong path to certain death!"

After he finished muttering those words angrily to himself, he suddenly froze. Wait!

Merlin had left clear directions.

Without hesitation he chose the right path, where the red marker was. Not a marker of death, but of freedom.

He felt his way along the wall, making his way deeper into the cave, determined to see this through to the end.

As he did so, occasionally his hand would brush across squishy, soft insects that burst from the contact. He resisted the urge to scream, but instead did his best not to hurt any of more, by keeping a lighter touch, thus making his journey even more difficult, even if more humanly kind. At least to the insects.

This would become a trademark of his personality in the future years. A man who cared even about the slightest of things in God's creation, though a bit arrogant when it came to his abilities at times, and a womanizer when he felt threatened or at a loss. All those at that time still lay far ahead of him. At that moment he just a child on a man's journey of self-discovery and exploration.

As he proceeded, he began to hear a soft singing, almost human, but not quite. It was utterly stunning and beautiful. If angels were made of stone, perhaps this is what their angelic voices would sound like.

Soon the voices grew louder, more insistent, almost urgent and then he took a hard turn and as he walked forward the passageway began to brighten, as if someone were dialing a flame up in a lantern.

Finally, it was so bright he had to shield his eyes with a hand to continue further.

He peeked between his fingers and saw he had come into a vast chamber filled with rainbows. And not just any rainbows, but rainbows of unimaginable colors, ranging from red to blue, yellow to brown, golden to violet and all the shades between and more!

He stopped. His heart had been pounding with excitement, but now it seemed to freeze as he realized where he really was. He had found Merlin's Crystal Caves. Really, really found them.

# Gentleman to the Rescue

*The Present.*

Harry was strolling down Chapel, enjoying the cool breezes of autumn when he heard a young woman's cry for mercy. The voice sounded full of fear and something else. Something familiar.

Help he would have understood immediately, but mercy was confusing to him.

He almost waited too long to seek the source of the voice, but when it came again it was in great agony. He winced at his reluctance and ran, using his cane to further his running steps, almost like a jumping stick the kids used in the parks.

He reached the alley of suspicion and plunged into it, heedless of self-danger.

She stood against the right wall, a tall man leaning over her, clutching a cross in one hand made of pure silver. It shone as he pressed it into her delicate neck, eliciting a new cry for mercy.

"Never!" He laughed. "You are a foul demon, and I shall not stop until your flesh returns to the earth from which it came."

The young woman in a move of desperation flung a fist into his face, which he caught with his other hand, which was holding something globule.

She screamed as her hand burst into flames.

"Oh, dear God!" Harry cried out despite himself.

He did not know for sure whether the man was a villain or not, but anyone who inflicted pain for pleasure was not the sort of fellow with which he could side.

He rushed forward with his cane thrust before him. "Unhand her, you beast!"

The man kept his cross pressed to her neck, which was beginning to smoke.

Her eyes rolled in pain, not even seeing Harry.

Harry's eyes narrowed.

"You will unhand her or pay the cost!"

The man laughed. "A mere lad such as you are but a fly on the wall of my life."

He moved his hand with the globule so fast that Harry could not move. The globule struck Harry on his chin and then tumbled to the pavement.

The man gave Harry a surprised look. "You're not one of t hem!"

"Oh, but if being one of them, means being one of you, I am most definitely one of them!"

Harry stabbed the man in his side with the tip of the cane with all his strength. The man uttered a cry of pain and turned away from the pinned woman to fight with Harry.

But Harry was not waiting for the man to strike back; he already had his left fist flying at the man's face.

The man grunted in pain as Harry's left connected with his jaw, sending him flying back against the wall next to the young woman.

She slid away from him, her left hand gripping her burnt neck and looked at Harry. "You would help a vampire?"

Harry gave her a surprised look, then a grin.

"I'd help the devil if he was as lovely and sweet as you, fair lady."

The man on the pavement swung his right hand out. Harry tried to grab it, but it was not an empty hand, it held a long blade. Harry recoiled in pain as the fallen man struck his left leg with the tip of the knife.

Harry winced in pain as the man swung again and made a new slice, but this time higher on Harry's thigh as the man regained his footing.

Harry swung his cane then with all his might at the man's head. He missed his head but struck the man's neck.

The man rolled away against the wall, clutching at his neck, and screaming in pain. He struggled to keep his feet as he backed away from Harry and the woman.

"You haven't seen the last of me!"

He ran off.

Harry smiled at the young woman. "Well, I certainly hope that's so, because next time I intend to dent his head quite thoroughly," Harry commented drily.

"You're brave," she told him.

Something about her face looked familiar.

He was about to ask who she was when he felt so faint, he could no longer stand on his feet. "I think I need to sit..."

Whatever clever words were about to breach Harry's lips subsided into a moan and he collapsed to the pavement and into a gentle oblivion of darkness.

# Magic and Illusions

*Some time back.*

"Shhh. Not a sound!" He whispered, his voice echoing throughout the theater, which had been acoustically modified to bounce his voice from one area to the next, amplifying it until it vibrated the bones of the ears of everyone listening. That caused their very bodies to vibrate, as if a gentle massage were being applied, and calmed them.

He needed to calm them. His next stunt was dangerous, even for him. He thrived on danger, not reckless danger, but danger that involved him mastering a challenger, or taking on a challenge he had yet to face and grow from.

Harry Houdini was the consummate escape artist and magician. He used his various skills to manifest an act of such profound terror and awe that the audiences sat spellbound through every minute, every second of it, some of them even fainting from holding their breath too long. Others piling on the popcorn, candy, and teas that the vendors who moved silently throughout the theater and sold.

That very side job was what truly paid him, not the theater tickets. Most of that paid for his helpers, the light engineers, the stage workers, the ticket takers, the manager, and the rent of the theater. He owed it. It was named "Magic and Illusions" after the very acts that he produced throughout the year.

Since he was as likely to go on an adventure or assignment with his Baker Street friends, he had created a career that could be hot sparked at a moment's notice to create more income for him and his people relished the time off they had in between job assignments, as he didn't hold back on sharing the monies freely with them. There were no poor people working for him, at least not after they had been employed for a time.

He hated poverty and its lack of medicine, the snide remarks, the dark consequences of mixing in with those of more. He had endured all those things until he had built a career that was magnificent enough, he could rise from his own poverty and then begin to spread his own abundance around to alleviate the suffering of others.

While he was wealth in laymen terms, he was not onerously wealthy. He did not have a home that was ten stories tall as some of the wealthiest did, nor have expensive imports and portraits painted by the greatest artists of his time. No, his home was a single-story dwelling with enough room to sleep in, plan his acts in... a cellar basement for that with two rooms for storage and invention...and four bedrooms, a dining room, a library, an exercise room, and a kitchen. It would seem like a lot to the poor of London, but not to a middle-class citizen, of which he was not. He prided himself on the simpler abode, for he often had guests, so the extra three bedrooms were as likely as not to be filled with either family or friends, or both.

His near Baker Street friends such as Watson and Holmes came to visit, but rarely stayed, but some of those who lived under the sea such as Captain Nemo, or in the clouds like Wells and Verne, they would come and stay sometimes for weeks or even months if they had an adventure together in London.

It kept his life full and rewarding. He had no woman in his life, he did not think it fair to involve them in the risks he constantly took on stage and in the battlefield of crime and adventure. Though he did have a sweetheart he saw infrequently, who someone kept true to him and steady in his affections, whom one day he just might settle down with and have little Houdini's.

He smiled at that as he clasped one muscular hand and arm after another on the rope and climbed into the gigantic bottle that looked like an enlarged wine bottle with a narrow neck he could only get through with significant effort. This was the sale of his act this time. He would submerge himself within the well of water of the giant bottle, have three chains tied to his ankles and feet, five metal balls, and his hands padlocked behind his back so he could not work his personal magic.

Oh yes, he smiled. He could do REAL magic, but he preferred the stage magic for the excitement of it, keeping the more ethereal magic for his adventures with the Baker Street fellows, or the occasional research he would do in the Orients for little known magics and fantasy elements he could incorporate into his act.

He would only use real magic when his life or that of another was in danger. Though he and Conan would sometimes use it to defraud charlatan psychics and wizards who claimed powers they did not to fill their bank accounts at the expense of those with broken hearts. They did not bother the ones that read palms and predicted marriages, and such, for they never overcharged, but the ones who claimed to be just somewhat short of gods, they had to be accountable. One way or the other.

So, in the course of time and years of learning he and Conan had made many friends, saved many a poor soul the loss of their fortunes, and been scorned as heathens and worshippers of the devil by the very people who did so.

Harry laughed inwardly as he reached the top of the bottle and turned to face the crowd. He waved his hands as he delicately balanced on the edge of the bottle to the cheer of the crowd, then waited as his crew hefted the balls and chains to the top of the bottle, in preparation for plunging them into the warmer waters and then he as well.

Outwardly he exalted at the pleasure he brought the audience, but inwardly, he was a bit nervous, for he had seen an old enemy in the audience this night. One he had not seen perhaps for five years. Time had not been this man's friend. He had never been a looker before, but on this night, he looked as dark as a devil. And no doubt as malicious and dangerous as before. The last time they had met, the man had tried to stake him in the heart, mistaking Harry for a demon of the night...a vampire.

He laughed inwardly. Vampires were not demons, but modified humans with a touch of magic mixed into them from Elvin heritage.

Harry had ended up in the hospital for a month from the wound, which only the skilled hands of Doctor Watson and the dear Madame Curie had been able to preserve him.

He had discovered the whereabouts of the scoundrel, and then used his real magic to send him off to a side realm...a parallel world where his kind could prosper with fellows of a like mind. Some might call that cruel and unusual punishment, but he did not think it was cruel to offer a man who had tried to murder him because of his misguide religious beliefs a way to redeem himself. He had given the man a path back to their London, but only if he were to change his ways.

But tonight, as he looked out into the audience for the man, and remembering that look, he knew the man had not changed at all. This was unfortunate. For both him and Harry.

No matter. Each challenge on its own merits he thought as he slid into the water feet first, the balls and chains collapsing to the bottom of the bottom and pulling him to follow.

In moments bubbles of air began frothing to the surface of the bottle as he squeezed through by squeezing through its narrow neck. He would not be able to come out as easily, for the pressure of the water and its viscosity would cause his body to swell somewhat because of its warmth and he would have to painfully squeeze back out after unhinging his shoulder blades, which would cause him remarkable pain...at least until he moved them back into their proper orbits once more.

His crew corked the bottle with a jazzy looking cork that was sparkly and gorgeously decorated to offset the danger of what he was doing. For it was dangerous. Extremely.

He heard his announcer, Jacob Marley, tell the crowd. "From the moment we corked Harry Houdini into the bottle he will have only seventy seconds to escape the bottle. His ability to hold his breath is no more than seventy seconds.

We pray he shall prevail so we can all applaud him and come again for another night of thrills and chills in the House of Magic and Illusions."

Harry's cue had been spoken. He began twisting and pulling, unhinging his wrists so he could slide the padlocks from them. Once dropped, he carefully began to raise his feet one at a time and working on the balls and chains. There were three on each leg, so it took him another twenty seconds to do each leg. He had used fifteen seconds already for the announcement and removing the pad locks. He now had twenty seconds of air left and already he could feel his lungs straining to not let go what precious oxygen he had left and suck in the water for air instead.

Outside Jacob announced, "Nineteen seconds. Eighteen Seconds."

Harry kicked free the last of the balls and chains, straightened up and hinged his arms and legs properly again as he wriggled towards the cork to free it.

"Nine seconds. Eight seconds." Jacob's voice droned outside the bottle.

Harry smiled. Piece of cake. He lifted his hands and pummeled the cork. It had taken him five seconds last time, and he still had seven.

"Seven seconds."

Harry pummeled the cork again, but it did not budge.

Must be the extra curry I had for breakfast this morning he thought to himself, then still smiling pummeled the cork again, even harder.

He could feel his lungs on the verge of exploding.

Spots were beginning to form before his eyes.

"Two seconds."

The cork would not budge.

The crowd in the theater rose as one in horror, hands holding each other, clenched to mouths, looks of horror as Harry appeared to be unable to get free.

Harry started to panic. He was out of air.

The old enemy in the audience rose from his chair, a look of satisfaction on his face as he saw Harry's look of terror and his thrashing to get out.

"Good-bye, old friend." He muttered as he turned to leave.

As he did so he came face to face with Sherlock Holmes and Watson, behind them was Inspector Bloodstone.

Harry suddenly froze in the bottle, closed his eyes, then as effortlessly as a seal sliding through a hoop, stepped through the glass of the bottle onto the stage, his whole-body dripping water. He began gasping for air. His crew rushed forwards to drape him in warm cloth, and then lead him towards the backstage as the audience broke into thunderous applause.

"You are under arrest for the attempted murder of Master Magician and Illusionist, Harry Houdini." Inspector Bloodstone said sternly.

The old enemy snarled and broke free, running for the stage, drawing a pistol as he fled the law. "Die Harry! You foul heathen and offense to God!" He cried out and fired, the same time as Watson and Holmes fired their own weapons.

The old enemy snapped backwards, and then collapsed.

On the stage, Harry dropped the cloths about him, turned around smiling and revealed a smoking bullet in between his fingers.

The audience, thinking the death was staged, broke into thunderous applause, yelling and screaming their love for him.

Harry, however, was not happy. He had tried to save a soul and it had not worked. Some just would not change no matter how many chances they were given.

He dropped from the stage and felt his old enemy's throat for a pulse, then motioned to his helpers, who came down and covered him with cloths.

"Magic and Illusions." He uttered to the dead man. "That's all I am. Magic and Illusions. But you had life and breath. Now...not even that. May God have mercy on your soul."

He turned around and climbed back onto the stage to prepare for his next act. His friends had used his act to help him catch the man, but instead all had gone wrong. He had much to think about where he had gone wrong in his own actions, to allow this soul slip through into a self-made hell.

Sadly, he left the stage. Sadly, he went to his stage room to ponder the meaning of his life. Such was the life of Harry Houdini that night.

# Plight of a Fallen Man

Somehow, through the fog of pain and unconsciousness, Harry felt strong hands, and then arms wrap about his legs and chest. Then he felt as if he were lighter than air.

He had never felt such exhilaration before. It was magical, as if he were flying.

Somehow, he managed to fight his way through the waves of pain and darkness to momentarily open his eyes.

He should never have done so. He must have been delirious, thinking that he was being carried, for he was not at all being carried, but instead he was falling.

Not flying at all but plunging face down towards an exceptionally large building below from a great height. He opened his mouth to scream, but then mercifully he lost consciousness yet again as he felt a gentle prick on his neck.

Page |

# Don't miss out!

Visit the website below and you can sign up to receive emails whenever John Pirillo publishes a new book. There's no charge and no obligation.

https://books2read.com/r/B-A-EMSD-PGABC

**BOOKS 2 READ**

Connecting independent readers to independent writers.

Did you love *SHERLOCK HOLMES, URBAN FANTASY MYSTERIES 2*? Then you should read *The Baker Street Universe*[1] by John Pirillo!

[2]

"I am dying!" Conan said to the Stranger who had come to him.

"No, you are not!" Professor Challenger told him. "This is just the beginning!"

In Victorian London, a doctor is dying.

And not just any doctor...but the late, great Sir Arthur Conan Doyle!

*Before he passes on, he wants to make sure his wife is taken care of...*

*Shown just how much he truly loves and cares for her...*

*And finish his last Sherlock Holmes story, which will be his masterpiece!*

---

1. https://books2read.com/u/bx1k0q

2. https://books2read.com/u/bx1k0q

And in another Victorian London, existing on a parallel world in a parallel universe to ours, there are heroes, heroes who exist in a world of magic and Steampunk science.

*They have other plans for Conan.*

*To rescue him.*

*From death!*

A deeply moving portrayal of the late Sir Arthur Conan Doyle which digs deeply into the lore about him and connects him intimately with the very characters he's written in a new universe...one of many which parallel our own.

Conan is going to be given a choice few of us are ever given...

The choice to pass on from life or to continue living...

*In another universe...*

*The Baker Street Universe!*

*Where he has the chance to be part of the Sherlock Holmes team and to make friends who are true heroes, just like the ones he has written.*

*And even more exciting for him is the knowledge that if he does cross over into this new universe, he will be alive during the most exciting time of history!*

*Every writer that ever lived.*

*Every character that every writer has ever written.*

*All will be alive and existing in this parallel universe!*

An Urban Fantasy Sherlock Holmes mystery novel.

Take a heartwarming and fun ride through the minds of Sir Arthur Conan Doyle, Sherlock Holmes, Watson, and so many others you have read about, but never seen in such vivid detail.

**Buy your book now.**

Read more at www.johnpirillo.com.

# Also by John Pirillo

**Angel Hamilton**
Broken Fangs


**Baker Street Universe Tales**
Baker Street Universe Tales
Baker Street Universe Tales 2
Baker Street Universe Tales 3
Baker Street Universe Tales 4
Baker Street Universe Tales 5
Baker Street Universe Tales Seven


**Between**
Prince of Between


**"Classic Baker Street Universe Sherlock Holmes"**
Sherlock Holme: Hyde's Night of Terror
Case of the Deadly Goddess
Case of the Abominable

**Detective Judge Dee**
Detective Dee Murder Most Chaste

**Elektron**
Elektron

**Escape To Adventure**
Escape to Adventure

**Hollow Earth Special Forces**
Hollow Earth Special Forces, Forbidden World

**Holmes**
Sherlock Holmes Struck
Sherlock Holmes A Dangerous Act

**Mystery Knight**
HellBound Mystery
Hell Bound Angel

**PhaseShift**

PhaseShift
PhaseShift Two: Crossover
PhaseShift: Shifting Worlds


**Rocketman**
Rocketman
Rocket Man, Mission Berlin
Rocketman Christmas
Rocket Man, Sky Commando
Time Wars


**Sherlock Holmes**
Sherlock Holmes, ICE
The Ice Man
Sherlock Holmes Fallen
Sherlock Holmes: Monster
Sherlock Holmes: Tick Tock
Sherlock Holmes Christmas Magic
Sherlock Holmes Dark Secret
Sherlock Holmes Shadow of Dorian Gray
Sherlock Holmes Vampire
Sherlock Holmes: Cursed in Stone
Sherlock Holmes Apparition
Sherlock Holmes Case of the Raging Madness
Sherlock Holmes Dark Princess
Sherlock Holmes Dark Angel
Constable Evans' Fancy
Sherlock Holmes Matter of Perception
Sherlock Holmes Tangled
Sherlock Holmes Case of the Gossamer Lady

Sherlock Holmes House of Shadows
Sherlock Holmes The Yellow Death
Sherlock Holmes Oblique
Sherlock Holmes Mystery Train Winter Collection
Sherlock Holmes A Tale Less Told
Sherlock Holmes Mystery Six
Sherlock Holmes, Rules of Darkness, Special Edition
Sherlock Holmes Shape of Justice
Sherlock Holmes Christmas Magic
Sherlock Holmes Fallen Angel
Ghostly Shadows
Sherlock Holmes: Artifact
Sherlock Holmes Bloody Hell
Sherlock Holmes Monster of the Tower
Sherlock Holmes Darkest of Nights
Sherlock Holmes Nightmare
Sherlock Holmes Poetry of Death
Sherlock Holmes, Dracula
Sherlock Holmes #3, Ice Storm

**Sherlock Holmes Urban Fantasy Mysteries**
SHERLOCK HOLMES, URBAN FANTASY MYSTERIES 2
Sherlock Holmes URBAN FANTASY MYSTERIES 3
Sherlock Holmes, The Dracula Files
Sherlock Holmes, Dark Clues
Sherlock Holmes, Case of the Undying Man
Sherlock Holmes, Mystery of the Sea
Sherlock Holmes, Night Watch
Sherlock Holmes, Mystery of the Path not Taken
Sherlock Holmes, the Dorian Gray Affair
The Baker Street Universe

Sherlock Holmes, The Dracula Affair
Baker Street Universe Tales 6
Spector

**The Baker Street Detective**
Strange Times, The Baker Street Detective, Book2
The Baker Street Detective, Hollow Man

**Standalone**
Sherlock Holmes Deadly Consequences
Invisibility Factor
Red Painted Souls
Between
Robin Hood
Shadow Man
The Rainbow Bridge
Cartoon, Johnnie Angel
Sherlock Holmes 221B
Sherlock Holmes Shape Shifter
Urban Fantasy Mysteries
Sherlock Holmes, Urban Fantasy Mysteries

Watch for more at www.johnpirillo.com.

9 798215 566312